The Arctic Challenge

BEAR GRYLLS ADVENTURES

The BEAR GRYLLS ADVENTURES series

The Blizzard Challenge
The Desert Challenge
The Jungle Challenge
The Sea Challenge
The River Challenge
The Earthquake Challenge
The Volcano Challenge
The Safari Challenge
The Cave Challenge
The Mountain Challenge
The Arctic Challenge
The Sailing Challenge

The Arctic Challenge

Bear Grylls

Illustrated by Emma McCann

X Bear Grylls

First American Edition 2021
Kane Miller, A Division of EDC Publishing

First published in Great Britain in 2019 by Bear Grylls, an imprint
of Bonnier Zaffre, a Bonnier Publishing Company
Text and illustrations copyright © Bear Grylls Ventures, 2019
Illustrations by Emma McCann

For information contact:
Kane Miller, A Division of EDC Publishing
PO Box 470663
Tulsa, OK 74147-0663
www.kanemiller.com
www.usbornebooksandmore.com

Library of Congress Control Number: 2020941130

Printed and bound in the United States of America
1 2 3 4 5 6 7 8 9 10

ISBN: 978-1-68464-236-6

*To the young survivor
reading this book for the first time.
May your eyes always be wide open
to adventure, and your heart full
of courage and determination to
see your dreams through.*

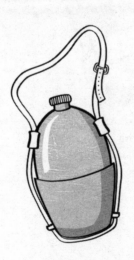

1

LEFT AND WRITE

Joe laughed, excited and dizzy, as the world spun around and around. It was just like being inside a washing machine.

He was strapped inside a huge transparent plastic bubble, with his friend Omar, bouncing around a sandy track. This was the Bubble Run, one of camp's many activities. Joe could see the other bubble trundling behind them, with Lily and Mia in it.

"Turn coming!" Omar called.

"I see it," Joe said confidently.

To steer the bubble, they both had to lean in the same direction at the same time.

"And … lean!" said Omar.

The bubble rolled around the turn, but they were going a bit too fast and it overshot, straight into a tree.

They bounced off and Omar and Joe laughed. This was fun! But Omar spotted a problem.

"Hey, we're going to hit the girls! Lean left!"

2

Deliberate
bubble bumping
wasn't allowed.
It spoiled the fun for
everyone. Joe leaned.

"No, *left!*"

Joe quickly leaned the other
way. Too late. The bubbles bounced
off each other.

"We've got to get out of their way,"
said Omar. "Lean right."

Joe felt his brain jam up. Right, left,
which was which?

3

"Right!" Omar urged. "Come on, Joe, or we'll hit them again!"

The girls' bubble thumped into theirs again. Omar saw where they were rolling in alarm.

"We're right at the top of the slope! Lean left …"

Joe panicked. It was too late. The two bubbles were out of control.

For a few dizzying seconds, the whole world whirled as they bounced down the slope. The bubbles stopped at the bottom with one last bump. With their heads still spinning, they unstrapped themselves and clambered out.

Everyone was dizzy and a bit dazed, but Joe was relieved to see that no one looked hurt. Well, almost. Lily looked slightly more confused than the others.

Joe was going to say something, but then a leader came running down, a look of worry all over her face. She asked if everyone was okay, and Joe had to admit that it was his fault.

"Omar was telling me to go right but … uh … I just get muddled …"

Joe expected everyone to laugh, but no one did. The leader just gave a sympathetic smile. She pointed out that Joe and Omar both wore watches on their left wrists – so from now on, Omar should tell Joe "watch" and "not watch" instead of "left" and "right." They pushed their bubbles back to the top, and finished the Bubble Run without bumping out of control again.

But the fun had gone out of it for Joe. He just felt silly.

Afterward, they were all at lunch with the rest of camp in the dining clearing. They picked a table in the shade of a tree. Joe let the others chat while he studied his hands. He *had* to get this right.

Once, for one day only, Joe had tried marking his hands, "L" and "R." Then someone noticed the "L" and asked what it was for. He had made up some excuse, and gone straight off to the bathroom to wash the letters away. It was just embarrassing.

"Watch" or "not watch" should work. As long as he always wore a watch, and remembered which wrist to put it on. But, apart from Omar,

7

people would just keep on saying "left" and "right."

Joe used to have an easy way of remembering directions.

Left was the way you turned out of his house to head for town.

Right was the other way.

This had worked for him, until a teacher at school had tried to be helpful.

"Your *right* hand is the hand you *write* with, Joe!" she had said with a smile.

She hadn't noticed Joe was left-handed.

So now his thoughts went something like this:

Left is *town direction* which is *this* way, but that's my writing hand and I *write* with my *right* except I don't I write with my *left* and … AARGH!

That was when his brain sort of locked

up. There was just too much thinking going on up there.

And that was how it had been for him ever since.

"Hey, Joe." Lily interrupted his thoughts. "Maybe you'd like this?"

She pushed a compass across the table at him.

Joe wondered if she was trying to be helpful, or if she just thought she was being funny.

"Why do you think I need a compass?" he demanded. "Because I get lost so easily?"

"No, it's not that," she said. "Really. Just consider it a gift."

Joe could see that Lily was serious. She really was giving him a present.

"Okay. Uh … thanks?" Joe put the compass in his pocket. Maybe it would come in handy.

Meanwhile, Mia was still trying to say that the crash hadn't been her fault, even though it turned out that she'd not strapped herself in correctly.

Joe fought back a sudden wave of irritation.

He wanted to yell, "It wasn't *all* our fault!" But anything he said might just remind people that he couldn't tell left and right.

Abruptly, Joe stood up. Omar looked up in surprise.

"Hey, Joe, you haven't eaten."

"That's okay. You have it," Joe said. "I just need to … go somewhere."

Omar looked anxious.

"You sure you'll be okay?"

Joe realized his friend was looking out for him. Omar was worried Joe would get lost.

"I'll be fine," he said, turning away. "I've got a compass."

2

NO DIRECTION HOME

Joe slouched through the trees, kicking at the leaves, hands in pockets.

"Dumb, dumb, dumb," he muttered.

But he knew he wasn't dumb. Not really.

Joe had a friend at school with reading challenges. His friend wasn't dumb either. Some kids found math hard. Some kids couldn't play a musical instrument. Joe got confused about directions. It didn't make any of them dumb.

The only person telling Joe that he was dumb was Joe himself.

But it was just so annoying!

And he was hungry. Joe's stomach rumbled, loud enough for anyone else to hear. If there had been anyone around. There wasn't because Joe had wandered deep into the woods. He couldn't hear any of the sounds of camp.

Joe sighed. It *was* dumb to be hungry when you didn't need to be. He should make his way back. Maybe he could get there before the end of lunch.

Joe turned around – and stopped.

Which way?

Joe set off through the gap between two trees. He had come this way ...

Hadn't he?

Or maybe he had come from over there, past that bush?

Joe rolled his eyes. Yup, he had managed to get lost again.

Normally, Joe made sure he went everywhere with his friends. They all just stuck together and he didn't have to think about directions.

He'd managed to get himself lost at camp once before, and accidentally won a game of capture the flag. But nothing good was going to happen accidentally now, he thought glumly.

Then Joe remembered the compass. He pulled it out and studied the dial. Four directions, one needle, always pointing north. Easy. He just had to follow the needle …

But which direction?

Joe groaned out loud.

He had no idea where the dining clearing was. So, he had no idea which direction to follow.

And he was still hungry.

"Well, that was clever, wasn't it?" he muttered.

Joe put his hands on his head, and thought.

There were paths and tracks running through the woods. There were lots of clearings. And there was a fence around camp. So, if he just picked a direction and kept going, then sooner or later he would find *something*. Maybe another kid. Maybe the fence. If he found the fence, then he could just follow that and he would find the main gate.

Joe picked a direction and started walking with a determined stride.

But after a while he had to walk around some bushes and then he couldn't see where he had come from.

Joe carried on, a bit more hesitantly.

Then he had to take a detour to cross a stream.

Now which way had he been going?

Joe felt his heart and breathing start to speed up. What if he just went around and around in circles in the woods forever?

The compass could help him head in a straight line!

Joe shot another look at the dial.

"Oh, what?"

So much for that idea. The needle was just going around and around. And instead of four directions on the compass, there were five.

"Fine, great, whatever," Joe muttered through his teeth. He stuffed the compass back into his pocket.

"So, next idea?"

Joe stared at the nearest tree, like it might make a helpful suggestion. Once, he'd heard someone on TV saying that trees could help you tell your direction.

But he couldn't remember how.

Joe turned in a slow circle and tried to remember what it was about trees and directions. It just wasn't coming to him.

"Dumb trees," Joe groaned.

He stopped moving, but now he was dizzy and it felt like everything was spinning around him.

"Aargh!" Joe shouted in frustration.

He stumbled, and suddenly realized that it didn't just feel like the trees were spinning. They really *were* spinning. Around and around and around. The ground underneath him was shifting and spinning.

Joe dropped dizzily to his knees, before he fell over. A freezing wind blasted its way through the woods. Joe yelped and clutched his arms. He was only wearing a T-shirt, and his bare skin had turned rough with goose bumps. Joe shivered and his teeth chattered.

He realized he wasn't kneeling on earth and leaves.

He was kneeling on … ice?

Joe looked up.

He was on a slab of floating ice, in the middle of a river. Other lumps of ice jostled and bumped each other as they slowly drifted downstream. The river was wide and swollen. Trees on either side looked like Christmas trees, covered with snow.

The slab wobbled under Joe. It was longer than a grown-up's height, but it was only as wide as his outstretched arms.

There was no sign of camp, or the woods that Joe had just been walking in. And his shivers were becoming uncontrollable. If something didn't happen soon, he might just shiver to death.

"Hello," came a voice nearby. "Over here!"

Joe's head whipped around. A man was running along the snow-covered bank.

GO WITH THE FLOE

The man was dressed in warm, padded clothes, with a fur-lined hood. He wasn't far from Joe either, near enough that he didn't have to shout. At least, he wouldn't have had to shout if there wasn't an ice-packed river flowing between them.

The man stopped by a small tree. A blade flashed in his hand as he hacked at a slim branch.

"You can't swim in water this cold," he called. "You'll have to push yourself over to the bank. Take this."

The man jogged along until he was level with Joe, then threw the branch like a javelin. It hit the ice just in front of Joe.

Joe's numb fingers struggled to hold on to it. He tried to stand up. The ice wobbled again and he quickly dropped back to his knees.

"Don't stand," the man called. "Stay just as you are. You need to keep your center of gravity low. Just push gently. Make sure not to push yourself off the ice."

Joe nervously put the branch into the water. The ice started to tilt, but he felt the end of the branch touch the bottom. He put all his strength into his arms. The ice moved, the end of the branch stayed where it was, but soon Joe was leaning right out and the ice was tilting. He quickly pulled the branch back in. The ice splashed back to being level again.

Bit by bit, Joe pushed his piece of ice toward the bank. The movement warmed him up – a little. His teeth didn't chatter so much and his shivering had slowed down. But he still couldn't feel his hands.

"You're doing really well!"

Joe didn't dare look up, but it was good to know the man was still there, encouraging him.

At last the ice bumped against the bank. The man was right there. He held his arm out.

"And, jump!"

The ice started to rock again as Joe stood up, and he jumped without any delay. The ice shot away backward, but the man grabbed Joe and swung him onto dry land.

"Perfect!" he said, smiling. "You handled that so well. Now let's get you warm!" He pointed to a clump of trees nearby. "My camp's back here."

Joe's arms and feet were going numb as they hurried through the pine trees to a clearing. There, Joe saw the most beautiful sight of his life: a small fire,

crackling away, with a steaming metal pot hanging over it.

Joe crouched next to the fire while the man pulled things out of his backpack. A warm, padded coat and a pair of thick trousers. A thermal hat. Gloves. Thick socks. Fur-lined boots.

Joe tried to pull everything on over the clothes he was already wearing. His fingers were so numb that he couldn't get a grip.

"Here, let me help." The man held the coat while Joe slipped his arms into the sleeves. "Every second counts when you're fighting hypothermia."

"Wh-what's that?" Joe stammered through chattering teeth.

The man helped Joe do the coat up.

"It's when your body core gets so cold, it can't warm itself up again. Don't worry, you'll be okay. We acted quickly."

The man set the hat on Joe's head.

"It looks like I'm your guide out of here," he said cheerfully. "My name's Bear. Are you ready for some real adventure?"

"I g-guess s-so." Joe's teeth still chattered. He pulled the hood up. Now he was thoroughly wrapped in warm clothing. He wasn't getting colder, but there was still a chill deep inside him. "Thanks. I'm J-Joe. And I'm still c-cold."

"Let's run on the spot," Bear suggested. He demonstrated, and Joe ran with him. He felt a very faint flicker of warmth deep down inside his body.

"And do this." Bear started to wheel his arms around like a windmill. "It looks a bit odd, but it's a great way to drive the blood back into your limbs."

Joe swung his arms like Bear had shown him, for about a minute. His

fingers started to tingle with pins and needles, but soon he was feeling almost back to normal.

Meanwhile, Bear poured him a drink from the pot over the fire.

"Fancy a cup of hot pine-needle tea?" he asked. "It's full of energy and vitamins. It's just what you need!"

"Thank you." Joe took it gratefully. He didn't care what kind of tea it was, as long as it was warm. The heat from the cup soaked in through his gloves and warmed his hands. They sat on logs on either side of the fire, and Bear poured a cup for himself. Joe sipped his tea and felt the glow inside him growing stronger.

31

"Thank you for helping me," Joe said. "But, um, where are we, exactly? I was trying to follow a compass but I think I've gotten really lost."

"Compasses won't work up here in the Arctic," Bear agreed. "They point to the magnetic north pole, but we're so far north we're almost on top of the magnetic pole anyway. A compass would just go in circles." Bear sipped at his tea. "I was trekking to the coast when an ice dam broke and the river flooded. It blocked my path. Having to find another route has added a good twenty-four hours to my journey."

"Couldn't you get across it?" Joe asked.

Bear smiled as he shook his head.

"You've got the survival spirit, Joe! It's always important to explore your options. Water's really powerful, even when it's slow. A river like that one, flowing at seven miles per hour, could wash a house away, so I wasn't going to try it. And the cold would be too much. So I'm heading for an abandoned hunting lodge to spend the night in. It's by a lake, a few hours' walk from here."

"It's lucky for me you were here, then," Joe said thoughtfully.

Bear smiled.

"Well, that's true! Good things often happen when we least expect them to. I'd only stopped for a rest and a hot drink, but it was the right time and the right place to meet you."

Bear and Joe both took another sip

of tea. Joe felt the warmth inside him. Bear smiled and said, "We'll be doing this a lot. We need to be hydrated and warm, and daytime temperatures here can be down to minus twenty. I've got some provisions – but, of course, I only brought enough for one person and for a shorter trek! We can forage off the land. Survival is about finding ways of using nature, not fighting it. But I should warn you ..."

"It's going to be tough, isn't it?" said Joe.

Bear nodded.

"That's right. But we have the right gear, we know where we're going, and we've got a positive attitude. Most of all, we've got each other – a team. Everything a survivor needs."

Joe could feel himself relax. Bear obviously believed they could do this, and that meant Joe began to believe it too.

Until a thought struck him.

He had *really* better avoid getting lost in these woods …

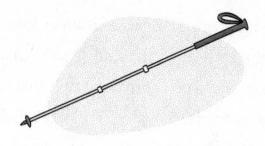

4

SNOW RIPPLES

As he helped Bear get ready for the trek, there was one question burning inside Joe.

They kicked snow over the fire, and Bear gave Joe an extendable walking stick. Joe adjusted it to his own height while Bear cut himself a fresh stick from a branch. Bear also passed Joe a one-liter water bottle to pack with snow while Bear finished working on his stick.

"That's great," Bear said when Joe had finished. "Put it in your coat's inside pocket, and your body heat will melt the snow into fresh water. We'll head due east and walk until the day warms up and the snow melts in the bottles. Are you ready?"

Joe nodded. He tried not to look nervous.

But as soon as they started walking, the question he'd been holding inside came bursting out.

"Bear, how will we know where to go? Which way is due east?"

"That's a great question. There are clues all around if we know where to look," Bear said. "For a start, we're following the way the wind usually blows – that's called the prevailing wind."

"But sometimes the wind changes direction," Joe pointed out.

"You're right, but 'prevailing' means that it *mostly* comes from one direction, just not always. Here, it mostly blows toward the coast, which is east. That's why this bush is thicker on one side than the other because it grows better away from the wind. Another sign is the moss growing on the trees." Bear tapped a trunk with his stick. "Do you see how it's only growing on this side? It's the side that the sun doesn't reach. In other words, the north side. With a bit of practice, you'll soon be able to work out the general direction."

"So, *that's* the thing with trees!" Joe said. He was determined to learn.

They kept going. Joe was still happy

to let Bear set the direction, but he kept an eye out for clues that they were still heading east. A couple of times his feet caught on tree roots and other things hidden beneath the snow and he stumbled. Bear showed him how to prod the ground with his stick before each step, to check.

Soon they came to the end of the trees. Joe stared. Ahead of them was a wide-open plain of snow, smooth and white. There was the occasional bush sticking up, and the odd tree. But Joe didn't think even Bear would be able to tell the wind direction from those. It was a lot of space to get lost in.

Bear seemed to know what Joe was thinking. He pointed at some mountains on the horizon.

"We'll be okay, Joe. Those mountains will make excellent landmarks. As long as we head for that big one, over there, we'll be going the right way."

"But supposing those clouds cover the mountains up?" Joe asked cautiously. He was so used to getting lost that he could generally see the flaw in any clever plan to stay on track.

"That's another good question." Bear pointed his stick down at the ground. "Look closely. Can you see that the surface of the snow is rippled?"

Joe peered at the ground. He had never noticed it before because the ripples were only about an inch high. And they were almost the same white as the rest

of the snow. But they were there, about four inches apart. They disappeared off into the distance, always pointing in the same direction.

"That's the prevailing wind again," Bear said. "These are called *sastrugi*, and the wind blows them all the same way. So, again, we have something to work out our own direction from."

Joe still kept one eye on the ground as he followed Bear across the snow, just in case the sastrugi all decided to wiggle around and face another way. They reminded him of the contour lines on maps, but that wasn't much comfort. Joe had never really gotten along well with maps.

The snow on the plain was deeper and thicker than in the woods. Joe followed Bear's example of lifting each foot well out of the snow before he put it down again. It felt weird, and it made his thighs ache. But it was less tiring than dragging his legs through the snow without lifting them.

After a while they approached a scraggly bush that was sticking up from the snow. It didn't look like much to Joe – just some bare stalks and a few withered leaves. But Bear knelt by it and poked some of the leaves apart. Joe crouched beside him and saw some small blue berries nestled together.

"Perfect. These are crowberries," Bear said. "In this cold we need twice the normal amount of calories to keep going.

These will top us up and give us a little
bit of vitamin C besides."

Bear started to pluck some. Joe spotted
a cluster of dark spots in the snow by
his knee. Some of the berries must have
dropped off already, he thought. Joe
fumbled to pick them up with his gloved
hands. Hmm. He held them up to his
face, to study. They didn't look exactly
like berries. More, sort of, leathery.

45

"And those would be reindeer droppings," Bear said with a smile.

"Yuck!" Joe quickly flung them away.

"It looks like the reindeer are going the same way we are," said Bear quietly. "See the tracks?"

The prints that trailed through the snow were shaped like two apple seeds, side by side – but much bigger. If Joe spread all his fingers out on one hand, he could just about cover an entire print.

"They're big!"

"Yup. They spread the pressure as

they walk on snow, to stop them sinking in," Bear said. "Now …"

The prints disappeared over a small rise, in the direction Joe and Bear had been heading.

"We'll go carefully," Bear murmured. "I don't want to have to go out of our way to avoid them, but reindeer have excellent vision and are easily spooked. Plus, they can run ten times faster than a human, so you don't have much of a chance if they decide you're a threat and charge you."

Joe and Bear crept forward and peeked over the edge of the rise.

There were the reindeer. A herd of about ten or twelve, the size of small horses, with reddish-brown fur. Some of them had massive, lethal-looking antlers sprouting from their heads. Joe was happy keeping a distance. He didn't want those heading for him, especially not if they were going to be traveling ten times faster than he could run.

Suddenly Bear cocked his head and held up his hand.

"Do you see that?" he whispered.

5

DEEP FREEZE

Joe squinted and looked. Bear pointed at a thick cluster of bushes at the bottom of the slope, but Joe couldn't see anything unusual. It was just a scrappy bunch of bushes.

But Bear was frowning.

"There's something there." He paused. "If it is what I think it is, we need to investigate."

Bear and Joe crept forward toward the bushes, but it was only when Bear parted some of the leaves that Joe saw it for himself.

A reindeer was caught up by its massive antlers in a tangle of branches and stalks. It lay slumped on the ground.

"Is it …?" Joe couldn't say the word.

"Dead?" said Bear, leaning down and placing his hand on its neck. "Yes. But not long ago."

Joe stared. He realized that this was the closest to a wild animal he had ever been in real life.

"How did it die?" he asked.

Bear pointed to one of the reindeer's legs. It was bent in a weird way. "It must have broken its leg and then gotten caught up in the bushes. It would have struggled for a bit. But out here, breaking a leg is a death sentence for an animal like this. It probably died of exhaustion."

"So what do we do?" Joe said.

"Well, this will feed a lot of other animals around here. It hasn't frozen yet, so it's really fresh."

Bear cut the antlers free of the bushes. Then he and Joe dragged the reindeer out into the open.

"Now we need to gut and skin it, before it freezes solid," Bear said.

"Gut it?" Joe asked.

"I mean, take out the stomach and innards. They go bad very quickly and they could poison the rest of the meat. Without them, the body will freeze naturally and be safe to eat for weeks."

Joe's jaw dropped as he realized what Bear was going to do.

"You mean we're going to eat it?"

"We're going to take enough to last us a day or two," Bear agreed. He smiled softly. "I know, it can seem harsh, but survivors can't afford to be sentimental. Taking food that becomes available saves us having to spend time and effort to get it later."

Bear cut a slit down the front of the reindeer, and pulled its fur apart. The innards were like stinky, rubbery bags all jostled together. Bear pulled them out onto the snow in a slopping, quivering heap that steamed gently in the freezing air.

"There's a small shovel in my backpack," Bear said. "Please could you dig a hole in the snow to bury these in? And then we'll dig another

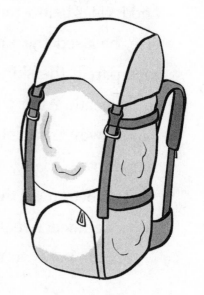

hole big enough to take the reindeer."

While Joe got to work digging, Bear started to remove the reindeer's fur.

"This is something else we can use. This guy's fur is perfect insulation. It could keep him warm in a minus fifty-degree winter, so it will do for us too. But I have to remove it quickly. Soon it'll be frozen and impossible to work with."

Bear left the fur on the reindeer's head, and its legs below the knees. Everywhere else, he used the knife and his fingers to separate the skin from the red flesh underneath. After a few minutes the fur came away completely, like a reindeer-shaped rug.

Then Bear used the knife to cut off one of the reindeer's rear legs.

"Fortunately we don't have to worry

about keeping this refrigerated."

"It will just freeze naturally," Joe realized.

"That's right! Now, let's get our friend buried, somewhere the predators can't get at him."

Between them, Joe and Bear dragged the reindeer over to the hole Joe had started and made it deeper.

"It's a shame we have to leave so much," Joe said, as they covered it up. "It seems like a waste."

"We can't take it," Bear agreed, "but maybe others will. We're going to mark this spot so that any other explorers who come this way will be able to find it – and so can we, if we need to come back."

Joe looked around. The endless waste of snow and ice looked back. There were no signs of humans anywhere. Suddenly Joe felt very lonely. He was extremely glad he had Bear for company.

"In a place like this," Bear said seriously, "you do what you can for your fellow explorers. Maybe we'll never know if we've helped someone today – but we will know we tried."

Bear cut a branch and jammed it into the ground. Then he tore a colored scrap of cloth from his backpack and tied it to the top, so that it fluttered like a little red flag.

"The best way to mark things in a place like this is with something that's obviously artificial. It stands out a mile."

Joe and Bear together folded up the fur. Bear opened up his backpack.

"Okay ... not enough room in here for everything now. Not with the fur and the leg. Do you mind doing some carrying?"

"Sure, no problem. But I don't have a bag."

Bear grinned. "Leave that to me."

Bear pulled out a tarpaulin and rolled the leg up in it. There were metal eyelets in the tarpaulin at each corner. He folded the two ends together and tied them together, with a piece of string threaded through the eyelets. Now the folded tarpaulin was a continuous tube. Bear looped it over Joe's arms and head, and folded it back behind his neck. Now the tarpaulin ran from under one arm, up over one shoulder, around Joe's neck and down under the other arm. Joe could feel the weight of the leg pulling his shoulders back. It wasn't anything he couldn't handle, and it all felt nicely balanced.

They took a drink from the water bottle. Sure enough, the snow had melted into cold, tasteless water.

Joe and Bear started to walk again, and after a few hundred yards, Joe looked back. He could still see the fluttering red scrap. It was the only splash of color in the whole landscape. Anyone who looked that way would see it immediately.

Well, Joe thought, maybe the reindeer meat would help someone else one day. He turned back to the way ahead, and his own problems.

There was still a lot of wilderness ahead to get lost in, he thought nervously. But, hey, maybe someone would have left *them* a marker too ...

6

PIECES OF THE JIGSAW

Joe and Bear trudged through a forest of silvery trees. Joe wasn't really sure what kind of trees they were, but he checked and saw that there was moss on some of them. Joe was still determined to get this navigation thing right.

He thought hard for a moment. If he and Bear were going *east*, and moss was on the *north* side, then the moss should be on the left. Or was it the right?

The first tree Joe looked at, he thought

the moss *might* be on the north side. It was on Joe's left, which was where north would be if they really were going east.

Next to it was a tree with the moss spread all over the trunk. Then there was a tree with no moss at all. The trees couldn't agree!

Joe must have made a frustrated noise. Bear smiled at him.

"Are you okay, buddy?"

Joe gritted his teeth and explained. Bear nodded, understanding.

"Well, it's like the prevailing wind. Moss is *mostly* on the north side, but it isn't always one hundred percent like that. Here's another one you can try."

A tree had toppled over. Bear pointed at the rings inside the trunk. They started in the middle and then grew larger as they got nearer the outside of the tree.

"A tree gets a new ring each year it's alive, during the growth season. But can you see here – the rings are slightly thicker on this side? That's because this side got more sun. So, that way is south. Of course, you need to find a fallen tree to see that one."

Bear stood up and held up his hands, with his fingers spread.

"So, you see, you can have lots of little clues. Moss. Rings. Wind. Plants. Sastrugi. They're all pieces of a jigsaw."

Then Bear clasped his hands so that his fingers were all linked.

"If you put them all together, nature gives you the big picture, and *that's* the one to look at."

Soon after that, they were walking

along a bank where the snow had piled up. Bear sunk his stick into the snow by a good three feet, and looked pleased.

"This is just what we need for our midday break."

"What, snow?" Joe asked in surprise. "Won't it be cold?"

Bear smiled. "You'll see!"

They used their gloved hands like shovels to dig out a trench in the powdery snow. Soon they had a hole in the side of the bank that was about three feet deep, and wide enough for them to sit side by side.

Bear scooped out one last little trench in the floor.

"This is a gutter for the cold air to sink into. Now, you look around for some branches we can put over this, and I'll make a fire."

Joe made sure he stayed within eyeshot of Bear as he walked off into the woods. Eventually, he found a couple of fallen branches. They were about his size and they still had leaves on them. Joe dragged them back to the trench.

Bear had lined the trench with the

reindeer fur, and built a fire in front. He and Joe laid the branches over the top of the hole, so that they could sit underneath them.

To Joe's surprise, he actually felt warm.

"So, we've got fur underneath us," Joe worked out, "and a roof to keep the warm air in."

Bear had made a small pile of fragments of the silvery tree bark next to the fire. He leaned forward and added another piece to the flames.

"And we've got a fire," Bear agreed

with a smile. "Birch bark is full of flammable sap, so it's perfect for the job."

So, now Joe knew what the trees were called.

Bear shaved some bits of meat off the frozen reindeer leg, and held them on a piece of wood over the flames to sizzle. They smelled, and tasted, delicious. They washed it down with more meltwater, and Joe filled the bottle up again with snow.

When they stood up again Joe got a chance to test his navigation skills.

"So, which way should we head now?" Bear asked, as he packed up the reindeer fur.

Joe finished kicking snow over the fire to put it out, and looked around. He pointed.

"That way?"

"Exactly!" Bear smiled. "What told you?"

"I just saw our footprints from where we walked up, and kept going in that direction," Joe said shyly.

Bear laughed.

"Well, that's another piece of the jigsaw! The obvious markers are the best, but you can still look for other clues if there aren't any. Like, do you notice that the tree branches on the west side are covered with snow, but not on the east?"

"Because the wind blows from west to east," Joe worked out, "so that's where the snow sticks."

"You've got it. You're really picking this up well, Joe."

Joe felt good for working out their

direction from the footprints. And he felt even better for Bear's encouragement.

After walking a few more minutes, they came to a frozen-over stream. The ice was thin enough to see the water moving underneath.

"We might have to cross this," said Bear, "but for the moment it's going in pretty much the right direction, so let's see what happens if we follow it."

Pretty much the right direction? Joe felt an immediate stab of anxiety. He could see with his own eyes that the stream wound back and forth between the trees. If they followed the stream then they wouldn't be heading due east anymore!

He tried to make himself calm down.

Okay, they were changing direction. But there would still be other clues.

They walked for a few minutes more, until the trees ran out. There were a few feet of clear ground, and then the stream ran right over a cliff.

The cliff didn't look high, Joe thought. Ten or fifteen feet. Still a bit too far to jump.

He started to walk forward, to see exactly how high the cliff was. Bear put a hand on his shoulder.

"Careful. We can't get too close. Do you see the way the snow is piled up along

71

the edge? I'll bet you it's overhanging the rock face. It will collapse if we stand on it – and it could fall on us if we tried to climb down."

Joe felt his spirits plummet. He looked back at their footprints, the way they had come.

"So ... do we have to find another way?"

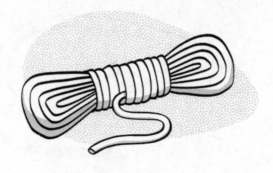

7

SUNNY SIDE UP

The one place the snow didn't overhang was the waterfall itself. Bear carefully followed the frozen stream to the edge and peered down. Then he smiled back at Joe.

"This is our way down."

He stepped back, and took a rope and a small ax from his backpack. Joe couldn't see anything they could tie the rope to. The trees were too far away.

Bear took the ax and bashed a hole into

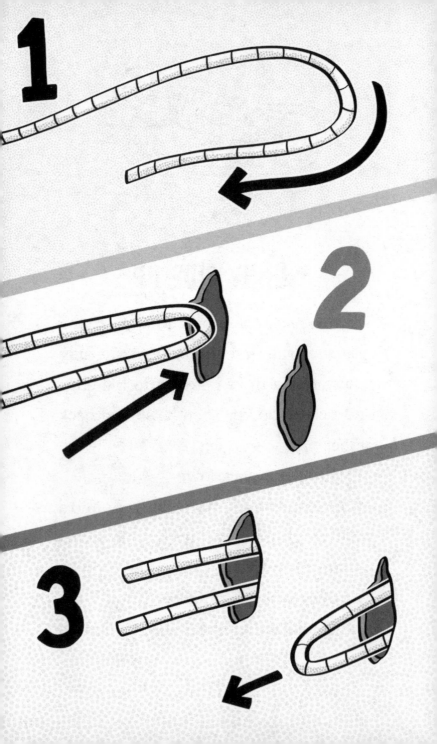

the ice itself. Then he bashed another, about three feet farther on.

Bear doubled the rope up into two parallel strands, and pushed the loop that joined them in through the top hole. He fished it out of the bottom one and kept pulling, until the two doubled-up pieces on either side of the holes were about the same length. Now he had four strands of rope in his hand, side by side – two going into one hole, two coming out of the other.

Joe started to understand.

"Now it's doubled up," he said, "so you just have to pull on one end and it will all come down after us."

Bear nodded.

"A rope's far too valuable to just abandon. And if we did it with just one length then our weight might make it cut through the ice so it won't hold us – but two strands should pad it out. I need to go first, to double-check that it's safe. Will you be okay coming down after me?"

Joe smiled.

"I get confused about left and right, but I think I can do straight down!"

Bear laughed.

"Great! Let's go, then."

First, they threw Bear's backpack and Joe's reindeer-leg sling down the cliff ahead of them.

"It makes us both slightly lighter, and nothing's going to break," Bear said. Then he took the four strands of rope in his hands and walked backward over the fall.

"There are rocks sticking out through the ice," he called up, "so double-check that there are plenty of footholds for you. Just never let go of the rope with one hand until you're holding it firm with the other. And only move one foot at a time."

A couple of minutes later, it was Joe's turn.

Joe let himself down, step-by-step, foothold to foothold. The ice creaked and groaned. He could hear the water trickling, and see it, a few inches in front of him, through the ice. The rope strands were taut with the strain of his weight. It was a relief when his feet finally touched the ground.

Bear pulled on one end of the doubled-up rope. The other end shot upward. A few seconds later, the whole rope dropped down at their feet. Bear coiled it up so that it could go back in his backpack.

While he did that, Joe looked around. He fought back a stab of worry. Did the stream still go the same direction as up above? He wasn't sure it did. So, how would they know which way to head?

Joe suddenly realized he had one massive clue to the direction they should take, right at his feet.

"We're heading for a lake, right?" he said. "And this stream must go somewhere …"

Bear smiled, and nodded.

"You're right, Joe. This stream almost certainly goes into the lake. All the watercourses around here will end up in it."

"So if we follow it, we'll get there!" Joe said happily. It didn't matter that the stream twisted and turned. If they followed it then they were absolutely guaranteed to get wherever it was going.

Soon the stream was flowing through a valley that wound and wiggled along. The valley sides were covered with bushes and small trees that stuck up out of the snow. Their stalks and twigs were dark and bare. But Joe noticed that one side of the valley was darker than the other because there were more bushes there. He bounced a few explanations around in his head. He could think of one right away.

"Is this the side that faces south?" he asked eventually. Joe pointed at the side with more bushes.

Bear nodded, with a smile.

"That's right, buddy. And the tree branches are longer, too. It's the side that gets more sun, so the plants get more energy. Did you spot that? You're turning into such a great navigator!"

Joe spent the rest of the trek gazing around, trying to take in more clues.

He was the one moving. *Nature* stayed still. The clues didn't shift around when he wasn't looking. He could trust the world to stay where it was.

He could do this!

Just as Joe was feeling confident, the valley ran out. The trees stopped, and the smooth surface of the frozen stream ran into a much wider, smooth surface of ice.

The lake!

The ice stretched away in every direction. There had to be a mile of it or more, before it reached the trees on the other side. Joe smiled to himself. They had walked for hours – most of the day, and the sky was turning red as the sun set. He'd learned to navigate and now they were right where Bear had expected them to be.

But the good feeling only lasted a second. Hadn't Bear said they were heading for a hunting lodge?

Joe looked around.

There was no sign of any kind of building. Just trees, and snow, and more trees, and more snow. All that careful navigating, Joe moaned to himself, and they'd still reached the wrong part?

"This *is* the lake, isn't it?" he asked, just to be sure.

Bear nodded.

"We're absolutely where we want to be, Joe," he said. "Come over here."

Joe trudged after Bear and tried to feel as cheerful as Bear sounded. Okay, it was the right lake. But where was the lodge, then?

That was when he noticed that a pile of snow by the trees had a metal chimney sticking out of it.

8

ICE AND FIRE

The chimney was the only clue. The rest of the lodge was just a smooth mound of snow.

"The door probably faces the lake," Bear said, "so we'll dig it out on this side."

He and Joe dug into the snow, like when they had made the midday trench, scooping out large chunks until they were both covered with white powder. A wooden wall slowly appeared, with a door, and a window of dirty, cloudy plastic.

"We'll leave the rest of the snow for insulation," Bear said, and pushed the door open. The inside was just as cold as outside, but at least it was snow free. The lodge was one big room. In the dim light, Joe saw a table and some shelves, with odds and ends on them. There was a metal stove, a pile of sticks and logs, and a couple of bunks.

Bear went straight to the stove. On the shelves next to it there was a box of matches, and an old newspaper left by a previous explorer. The pages were yellow with age, and bone-dry. Bear passed it to Joe.

"Joe, please could you tear up about a quarter of the pages? We don't want to waste the whole thing. Crumple them up into little balls."

While Joe did that, Bear grabbed a couple of armfuls of wood and built up a pile inside the stove. First, the paper that Joe had crumpled, then smaller pieces of wood on top of it, then a couple of logs on top of that. Once it was all in, he set fire to the paper with the box of matches. Yellow flames were spreading through the paper as Bear shut the metal door.

"We'll keep it fed while we're here, and we'll soon be warm and toasty!" he said. "And we can cook some more reindeer, too."

They drank melted snow, and fried some strips of reindeer meat in a metal pan on top of the stove. It tasted even better than their lunch. By now, the lodge

felt as warm as Joe's tent back at camp. They left the rest of the leg outside, in nature's freezer.

"Reindeer's fine," Bear said, as they washed it down with more pine-needle tea, "but we could sure use some fish for breakfast."

"Tasty!" Joe agreed.

"So, we're going to need some things. There's a ball of string in the backpack, if you can bring that. We'll be building another fire out on the ice, so we'll take these pieces of kindling and wood here, and replace them for other explorers before we leave tomorrow."

"Will the ice hold our weight?" Joe asked as they went outside. Once he had tried to stand on a frozen fishpond back home. He had gone straight through and gotten soaked. Out here, the result would be a lot worse. "The ice on the stream looked quite thin."

Bear smiled as he walked onto the ice and stamped his foot.

"The stream was moving, so it didn't freeze. Still water, in this temperature, will be fine. It needs to be at least two inches thick to hold your weight, but this will be more than that. If you're ever unsure, a good way is to give it a hard prod with your stick, three times. If it doesn't go through after that, it'll be okay."

Bear and Joe went out onto the ice for about fifty yards, with their arms full of sticks and logs and pieces of birch bark. Joe went back to get a second load of wood – a pile of spruce branches which

Bear had pointed out – while Bear started to cut a hole in the ice.

By the time Joe got back, Bear had used the ax and his knife to cut a hole in the ice as wide as a soccer ball. As Bear had promised, the ice was thick – Joe guessed four inches or more – and the water was dark.

"Could you pass me some string, please?" Bear said. He cut off a length about three feet long. Then he snapped a small twig off one of their pieces of wood, about half the length of Joe's little finger. With his knife, he cut away the bark and sharpened the two ends to points.

"Hold this, please?"

Joe held the wood while Bear tied the end of the string around its middle.

"This is called a gorge hook," Bear

said as he worked. He took the wood and the string, and held them so they were parallel. Then he pushed the pointed wood into a bit of reindeer meat so that one end came out of the other side.

"The fish comes along for a nibble, and gets the bait. But the bait is holding the hook parallel to the string. Without

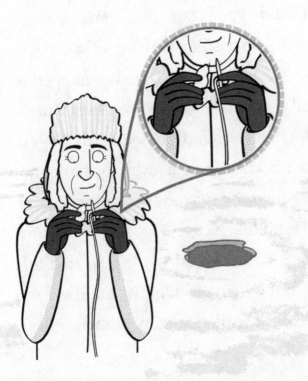

the bait, the hook swings around and catches in the fish's mouth, so it can't get free," Bear explained. "Now, the last thing we do is build a fire."

Bear and Joe made a pile of the sticks and pieces of wood they had brought, next to the hole. It started with lots of thin twigs and fragments of wood. On top, Bear put all the pieces of birch bark.

"While I get this going, could you gather up those spruce branches into a bundle?" Bear said. "We want all the leafy ends packed together. You'll see why."

Joe collected as much wood as he could while Bear set the fire alight. The flame took over the pile as the oils in the bark caught fire, crackling its way through the twigs and licking up against the bark pieces. Soon, orange flames rose cheerfully up into the sky.

Joe thought that maybe the fire was for them, to keep them warm while they waited for a fish to bite. But that seemed a lot of effort to go to, when they could just wait in their nice, warm lodge. He tried to think of nonobvious reasons, and got one.

"I suppose this attracts them?" he said. Joe imagined the glow of the flame from a fish's point of view, through the ice. Bear nodded.

"It's the brightest thing around, including underwater. They'll come to investigate, and find a nice bit of reindeer meat waiting for them."

Bear tied the string onto a stick, which he laid across the hole. The hook and bait disappeared into the water.

"And now the spruce branches ..." he said.

They packed the leafy ends of the branches into the hole around the fishing line. The branches pressed against each other, and against the side of the hole, so they stayed in place.

"And that stops the hole freezing over," Bear said. "You wouldn't believe how many ice-fishing trips have been wasted because people forgot to do that! Now, fish won't be the only creatures attracted to the fire. There are bears and wolves out here – so we should get back indoors. A night in the warm, and tomorrow we should reach the coast!"

9

ONE LITTLE FISHY

Daylight crept in through the grimy window. Joe stirred and stretched himself awake beneath the warm woolen blankets.

In the other bunk across the room, Bear was still asleep.

Joe's stomach growled. It reminded him of their plans for breakfast. Had they caught a fish?

It would be cool to go and see.

He pulled his outdoor gear back on, and laced up his boots. There was a pencil stub on the table. Joe scrawled a quick note on one of the pieces of paper: "going to check fish." Bear had said they were a team, and it felt like something a team member would do.

Joe was also thirsty. They could do with more water. There was an old metal water bottle with a leather strap on the shelf by the door, left by some other user of the lodge. Joe decided to fill it up with snow to melt. He slung it over his shoulder, pulled his hood up, and stepped outside.

He had forgotten exactly how cold it was outside until he felt it bite into his

exposed face. He gasped, and the air went into his lungs too. *Man,* that was cold!

Joe was glad he still had warm air inside his clothes and against his skin. He was well wrapped up in good Arctic clothing, and protected from the wind.

First things first. Joe scooped snow into the water bottle, and stuck it inside his coat, quickly, so as not to let the warmth out.

Then he walked down to the edge of the lake.

That part was easy. All he had to do was follow yesterday's footprints. Snow had drifted during the night and the footprints were faint, but they were still visible.

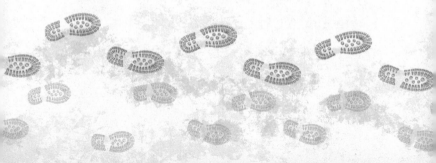

Then Joe looked out over the lake.

He couldn't see the other side. In fact, it was hard to tell how far he could see. A white mist hung over the ice. There was nothing firm to look at.

Joe stood and stared. He couldn't see any footprints, or the fishing hole. Not even the fire next to it. Joe knew it would have burned out long ago, but there should still be a pile of burnt wood and ashes.

All he could see was white, directionless mist. If Joe wanted fish for breakfast, he'd have to go into the mist.

Joe almost turned back. But then he looked down at the ice.

Sastrugi!

He hadn't thought to look for them the night before. He had just walked

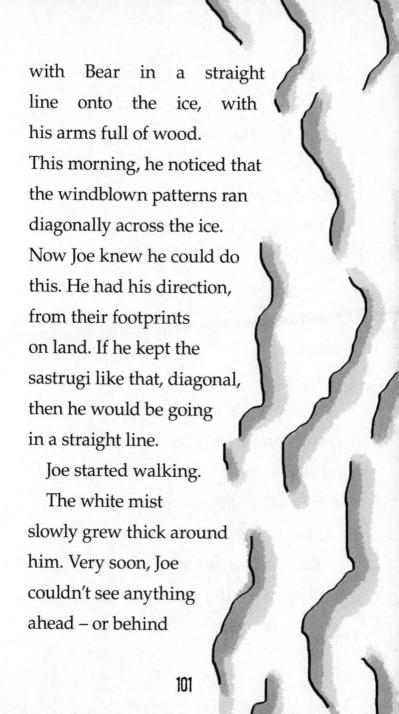

with Bear in a straight line onto the ice, with his arms full of wood. This morning, he noticed that the windblown patterns ran diagonally across the ice. Now Joe knew he could do this. He had his direction, from their footprints on land. If he kept the sastrugi like that, diagonal, then he would be going in a straight line.

Joe started walking.

The white mist slowly grew thick around him. Very soon, Joe couldn't see anything ahead – or behind him, either. The land and the trees had vanished into the white blur.

But he could see the sastrugi.

"Just keep walking," he muttered. "Just keep walking …"

Joe kept the sastrugi diagonal, and kept going.

A gray spot appeared in the mist. Dead ahead. Joe's heart started to beat faster.

And then he was standing by a pile of ashes, next to a hole in the ice stuffed with spruce branches. The fire had melted a small dip in the ice, but the ice was too thick for it to go all the way through.

"*Yes!*" Joe punched the air.

The spruce branches had kept the hole open during the freezing night. Joe pushed them apart to get at the fishing

stick with the line attached to it. The
line vanished into the water. Joe tugged
it between thumb and forefinger. It felt
like there was a weight on the other end.
Joe felt the excitement growing inside
him. He gave the line another tug.

There was a sudden yank on the other

end and the line was pulled out of his fingers. Only the fact that it was tied to the stick stopped it from disappearing into the water.

"We've caught a fish! Go, us!" Joe exclaimed.

He gave the line another tug, and this time he held on to it. He could feel the fish pulling against it, straining …

Suddenly, he realized what might happen. If he just kept yanking on the line, the fish would keep fighting back and the line would snap. The fish would get away and all that work would have been for nothing.

Joe gently let the line back into the water. That was close. Okay, so he didn't know what to do next. But Bear would. Now Joe just had to go and get him.

Joe knew that all he had to do was turn around and follow his footprints ...

Or did he?

When he'd gotten to the hole he'd walked around it. The ground was a blur of footprints. And the white mist worked both ways. You couldn't see where you were going – or where you had come from, either.

If he got this wrong, then he could spend the rest of his life walking around and around in circles on the lake ...

"Calm down, Joe," he muttered to himself. Whichever direction he went, he would come to land eventually. It wasn't going to move.

And he still had the sastrugi. They had guided him here, they could guide him back.

Joe made himself remember how the fire and the hole had been when he first saw them. He walked around, without taking his eyes off them, until they were in the same places again. Fire *there*. Hole *there*. Sastrugi going *that way*. So, he must have his back to the way he had come. Joe turned around on the spot, exactly half a circle. He made a note of which way the sastrugi were going now, and started walking.

A minute later, Joe was grinning from ear to ear. When he came out of the mist he was right on target. Joe followed his own footprints back up to the lodge, with a song in his heart.

Joe put his hand on the door to go in. Then he paused and took one last, satisfied look back. Everything was exactly where it should be, and that included him.

He turned back to the lodge and stepped in.

"Hey, Bear, we got a fish!" he called.

Joe stopped, blinking in surprise. Where was Bear?

In fact, where was the lodge?

The snow?

The lake?

Joe was standing on ground covered with dead leaves and pine needles. He was in his jeans and T-shirt and sneakers.

And he was *warm*.

10

A LOT OF BOTTLE

Joe was back at camp – but just as lost as he had been when he left.

He turned in a slow circle and looked at the trees.

He could see the moss, and the way the trees grew. He could make a stab at which way was south. But that didn't help if he didn't know which direction the dining clearing was in, did it?

"C'mon," he said quietly. "You can do this. Bear showed you how."

Part of him wanted to doubt it all. Joe knew he couldn't have gotten to the Arctic and back, just like that. He remembered how dizzy he had felt. It must be something to do with that. Something weird inside his head.

But he clearly remembered Bear telling him to look for clues. Maybe it was worth a try.

Joe thought back to his lunch with his friends. He closed his eyes and pictured it. They had chosen a table in the shade. It had been in a tree's shadow. So, the tree had been between the sun and the table.

He had walked away from the table, in the same direction as the shadow.

So, he had walked away from the sun.

Which meant that now Joe just had to walk *toward* the sun, and he would be back where he started!

Joe's heart pounded with excitement as he started to follow the shadows back through the trees. He was trusting himself to a dream. But somehow he felt confident. Even if he had dreamed it, it made sense.

Soon his ears told him he was on the right track. He could hear the sounds of kids having lunch, and he felt even more confident.

A couple of minutes later, he was back in the clearing. And there were his friends.

Even better, there was his lunch. No one had eaten it. Perfect! Joe felt extra hungry. He remembered how he'd walked all day and not even eaten the fish for breakfast.

Joe smiled and shook his head. *Not real!* he reminded himself. But even if it had just been a weird kind of daydream, his body seemed to *think* it had been real.

"Hi, guys." Joe sat down. Something was bumping against his hip so he pushed it aside. "Thanks for leaving my lunch."

"We were only half sure you weren't coming back," said Omar.

"So we only ate half your food," Lily said with a smile. Joe laughed.

"Thanks, everyone!"

But he didn't have very long to finish it. One of the leaders came along, clapping her hands.

"Okay, time for afternoon activities! And remember that two o'clock is the deadline for tomorrow's sign-up, so that gives you about ten minutes if you haven't already. No sign-up, no activity."

Joe ate quickly and got up to go. He still needed to put his name down for tomorrow.

Mia still had about half her lunch left and was chatting to Lily, seemingly unaware of the time.

"Hey, Mia, what are you doing tomorrow?" Lily asked.

"I haven't signed up yet. But it doesn't matter."

"You'd better hurry up then! You've got … eight minutes."

"Oh, it'll be fine, don't worry about it. I'll just decide tomorrow, and they'll sort it out for me."

"But if you don't sign up for something …"

"Look, Lily, it's just a silly rule. It doesn't really matter, okay?"

Mia was starting to sound annoyed. She never liked being told what to do, even when the rules were there for her benefit. She just wanted to do her own thing, even when it caused problems for other people. Somehow Mia just couldn't ever seem to admit that she was in the wrong.

Joe supposed he had been a bit the same with directions. People had tried to help him, but he'd just ignored them. He'd had a mental block about it. But then the adventure in the Arctic with Bear had totally sorted his head out.

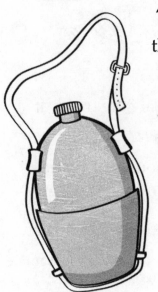

"Is that in case you get thirsty?" Omar asked as Joe caught up.

Joe looked down.

Hanging by a leather strap across his shoulder was a metal water bottle.

The water bottle Joe

had taken from the lodge in the snow, next to a frozen lake.

If this bottle was real then his Arctic adventure had been real too!

Joe looked back. Mia was still picking through her food.

"Uh, Omar – put my name down for tomorrow for whatever you're doing, would you? I just forgot something …"

"Okay, will do. See you in a bit."

Joe started walking back toward Mia. He wasn't sure what he would say when he got there, but he knew he had something important to tell her. Something that might lead her to Bear.

The water bottle bumped against his hip again – and against something in his pocket. The compass! Joe took it out and looked at it.

It just had the usual four directions. Somehow, though, Joe was certain that the compass was the answer.

Mia looked up at Joe cheerfully.

"Hi, Joe. Forget something?"

"Uh. No." Joe realized that she might think he was really weird. But it was a risk worth taking. He put the compass down on the table. "I just thought you might like this. You know. Consider it a gift."

The End

Bear Grylls got the taste for adventure at a young age from his father, a former Royal Marine. After school, Bear joined the Reserve SAS, then went on to become one of the youngest people to ever climb Mount Everest, just two years after breaking his back in three places during a parachute jump.

Among other adventures he has led expeditions to the Arctic and the Antarctic, crossed oceans and set world records in skydiving and paragliding.

Bear is also a bestselling author and the host of television programs such as *Survival School* and *The Island*.

He has shared his survival skills with people all over the world, and has taken many famous movie stars and sports stars on adventures – even President Barack Obama!

Bear Grylls is Chief Scout to the UK Scouting Association, encouraging young people to have great adventures, follow their dreams and to look after their friends. Bear is also honorary Colonel to the Royal Marine Commandos.

When Bear's not traveling the world, he lives with his wife and three sons on a barge in London, or on an island off the coast of Wales.

Find out more at **www.beargrylls.com**